I'm Glad
That You're
Happy

Nahid Kazemi

GROUNDWOOD BOOKS
HOUSE OF ANANSI PRESS
TORONTO   BERKELEY

Groundwood Books / House of Anansi Press
groundwoodbooks.com

We acknowledge for their financial support of our publishing program the Canada
Council for the Arts, the Ontario Arts Council and the Government of Canada.

Canada Council   Conseil des Arts
for the Arts   du Canada

ONTARIO ARTS COUNCIL
CONSEIL DES ARTS DE L'ONTARIO
an Ontario government agency
un organisme du gouvernement de l'Ontario

With the participation of the Government of Canada
Avec la participation du gouvernement du Canada | Canadä

Library and Archives Canada Cataloguing in Publication
Kazemi, Nahid, author
I'm glad that you're happy / Nahid Kazemi.
Issued in print and electronic formats.
ISBN 978-1-77306-122-1 (hardcover). — ISBN 978-1-77306-123-8 (PDF)
I. Title. II. Title: I am glad that you are happy.
PS8621.A94I4 2018   jC813'.6   C2017-907593-4
C2017-907594-2

The illustrations were done in pastel, color pencil and collage.
Design by Michael Solomon
Printed and bound in Malaysia

MIX
Paper from
responsible sources
FSC® C012700
FSC
www.fsc.org

To all the parents who are
best friends to their kids.

Our life together began on the day that Mr. Florist planted us in a rosy-colored pot. I was bigger and stronger, so he told me, "You have to take care of your little friend. It is smaller and weaker than you."

He placed us among
hundreds of flowers.
We opened our eyes
to their perfume
every day.

We saw many people who came to buy flowers.
They bought beautiful bouquets and gave them
to their friends and loved ones. They made their
friends happier and their houses more beautiful.

And one day, a kind man chose us from among the hundreds of potted plants in the flower shop.

In the street, as he held us in his arms, he pointed to the trees and said, "Look at these trees. You have the same future as them. I will take care of you. When you grow bigger, in the proper season, I am going to plant you in my garden."

Flower Shop

He took us to a colorful house. He was a painter, and he painted flowers and trees. We began our new life in that beautiful home.

Together we took part in all the events of the house. In times of happiness and at parties, when everyone was glad to be together, we were happy too.

We shared the sorrows of the people in the house, and we hugged each other in times of despair. We knew that we were growing up.

We grew bigger, and the pot
became smaller. Now there was
not enough room for us in the rosy
pot. Your roots couldn't breathe
properly, and you were sad.
You wanted to be in a better
place, and you were right.

Your despair made the kind
painter and me unhappy.
Finally, he decided to move
you. It was a difficult moment.
My roots were entwined in
yours. Leaving you was hard.

Hortus
organics

original
POTTING SOIL

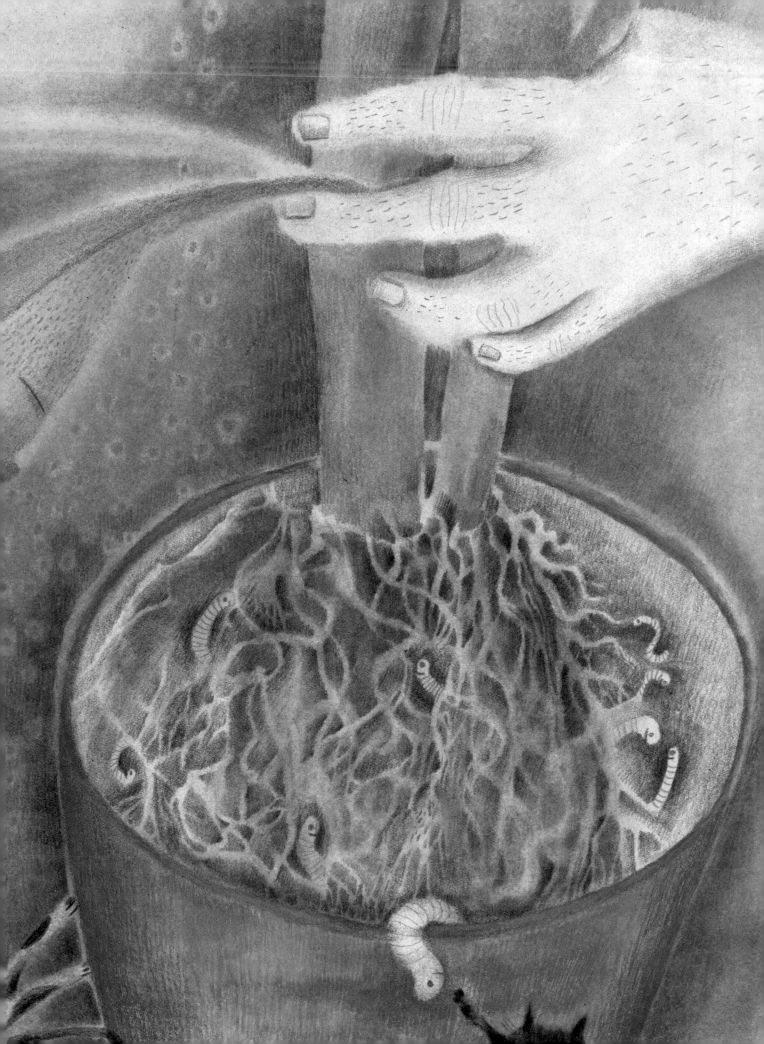

Now you are placed in the
corner of the painter's studio.
You have your own pot —
a bigger house — and you
can breathe more easily. You
have more leaves, and you've
become greener too.

I am in the corner of the dining room
now. I look at the pretty paintings that
the painter made of you. You have grown
up, and you've become more beautiful.

I am thinking of the day that
the kind painter plants us
in the garden, and we grow
into huge trees together.

I dream of the day
that sparrows sing
on our branches, and
children run under
our shade.